Charlie's Quest

Copyright © Stefanja Gardner 2022

Written by
Steffi Gardner

ISBN 978-1-914485-10-7

First Published September 2022

Printed in Great Britain by www.designmarque.co.uk

Other books from Steffi Gardner

Non fiction books

For Love of Harry
Life with Harry

Children's fiction

Charlie to the Rescue

To contact the author,
email: steffig@gmx.com

To: Olivia
&
Henry .

Charlie's Quest

Steffi Gardner

Best wishes
Steffi G.
Enjoy

Dedication

This book is dedicated

To Janine Lyford and Teg, with many thanks for all your help

Also to all SARDA volunteers

and their wonderful dogs.

You are all an awesome bunch –

Not forgetting the courageous dogsbodies

who may be shivering

in the cold for hours while they wait

to be found.

Thanks also go to Lynn Stuart for her delightful sketches.

Charlie's Quest

QUEST

A long search for something that is difficult to find

or an attempt to achieve something difficult.

He was going to be a Search and Rescue Dog. That's what he was going to be. He'd decided that the moment he found Rosie and felt his heart swell with pride, his spirit ancestor there beside him. After all, how difficult could it be?

What he didn't know of course is that many quests are not easy, in fact some almost impossible to achieve. And those taking part have to change and adjust along the way in one way or another. Also, that a successful quest can take a long time – to people at any rate.

Will Charlie succeed? Or is it a dream that disappears in the light of day? I wonder! Shall we see?

CHAPTERS

Chapter One 9

Chapter Two 13

Chapter Three 19

Chapter Four 23

Chapter Five 25

Chapter Six 29

Chapter Seven 33

Chapter Eight 37

Chapter Nine 41

Chapter Ten 47

Chapter Eleven 51

Chapter Twelve 55

Chapter Thirteen 57

Chapter Fourteen 61

Chapter Fifteen 65

Chapter Sixteen 71

Chapter Seventeen 73

Chapter Eighteen 77

CHAPTER ONE

Charlie lay in his basket a mutinous expression on his face. It hadn't been his fault. His spirit ancestor, some would say 'guide', was wrong. Charlie sulked. It wasn't his fault he said to himself. 'IF ONLY.'
Life was made up, he thought, of a series of 'IF ONLY'S.'

If only he hadn't smelled that mysterious smell he couldn't identify but which he had to, just had to, find

If only Bob hadn't left him in the garden when he went to answer his 'phone

If only the delivery man hadn't forgotten to close the gate

If only 'someone' had stopped to think

If only 'someone' hadn't ignored Bob's call and Megan's bark

If only 'someone' hadn't dashed through the gap between the delivery man's legs.

There were other 'IF ONLY'S' of course. Like 'If only' a certain 'someone' had stopped at the kerb. Added to that if only there had not been two cars on the road when 'someone' dashed into it. If only the car that hit that 'someone' had swerved, guess who wouldn't have ended up at the vets? I'm sure by now you will have worked out the name of that four legged 'someone.' If none of this had happened then that certain someone, Charlie, would not be stuck here in his new home with a badly bruised leg.

Now Border Collies are said to be very bright clever dogs and, of course, they are, as are most dogs. Charlie though was still young and had a lot to learn, including accepting when he was wrong.

Bob sighed. Charlie, with one ear up and the other down, was gazing at him and Megan with such soulful eyes, almost as if saying forgive me, please forgive me. What could you do with a dog who gazed at you looking pathetic? Charlie's tail thumped and he licked Bob's hand as his new guardian bent forward to stroke him. From her bed Megan yawned then woofed as if to say 'talk about being lucky.'

Later that night just before he went to sleep and had time to think, Charlie grudgingly admitted he had been wrong. It was his fault. He remembered the cry and look of panic on Bob's face when he dashed into the road and scooped him up. How he had felt Bob's heart race. How he had called the dog's name, pain and panic in his voice. All this within the first forty-eight hours of being in his new home too - within minutes of exploring his new garden with Megan.

Curiously, as he admitted to himself it was his fault, he felt something inside him relax. It was as if in accepting it was his fault a part of him had grown. It was very strange. Physically he had not altered. He was still seven months' old yet somehow he felt older and stronger for owning up.

Bob knew that Charlie as clever as he had been to find Rosie, when the dog was still living with The Jenkins, was still unsocialized and untrained. He had known the dog had a mind of his own. Finding Rosie had proved that. Charlie had gone against what Mr. Jenkins had said and in so doing had been the first to find her.

Now Bob wondered if he had taken on too much. Just forty-eight hours and already the dog was in trouble. He had wanted Charlie so badly, fallen in love with him even before the dog had found Rosie. Bob thought had he really stopped to think of all the steps that had to be taken?

On the drive to North Wales he had been thinking of the time Charlie would be a fully certified Search and Rescue dog. He had been so full of his plans but that was the future and! He needed to think one step at a time. This had to be at Charlie's pace and not his own. It had been so long since he'd trained a puppy he himself needed to go back to basics.

Lying in his basket Charlie looked so young and vulnerable. Bob made a decision that no matter how long it took he would not let Charlie down. He thought about the difference between the two dogs. Megan had always been biddable, whereas Charlie appeared to do first then think afterwards.

He remembered reading that a really good Search and Rescue dog did think for itself, and sometimes act against what the handler might demand. How could he have forgotten it was this characteristic he could see that had attracted him. It was this very quality that would eventually put Charlie ahead of the rest. But we're getting ahead of the story and that will not do! Earlier at the vets Mr. Chalmers had said 'already in trouble Charlie and in less than forty-eight hours. Hope we don't see you again for a long time'. He continued 'though I have a feeling we might be seeing you on a regular basis.' 'Hope not' said Bob.

At home curled up in his bed in the kitchen Charlie was warm, well fed and sleepy. The shock of the accident was starting to fade from his mind. Bob had given him a few drops of a well known remedy that helped to settle the emotions after a shock or trauma, Rescue Remedy it was called and often used both for people and animals in this sort of situation. It didn't matter how long ago the trauma had happened. The remedy was beginning to work on Charlie.

CHAPTER TWO

As he drifted off to sleep he thought again of arriving at his new home.

'We're home Charlie'. Bob opened the boot and took out a suitcase, rucksack and walking boots etc. then went round to let the dog out, clipping on the lead.

Charlie looked around him and sniffed before jumping down. The last hour of the journey he had been alert. The car windows had been open and he had closed his eyes breathing in all the new smells.

His two nostrils working independently of each other were full of scents.   On the breeze he sniffed and thought that's an animal. But what was it? It wasn't cow, it wasn't sheep. He knew those smells well. He could hardly wait to explore. 'Let me out, let me out' he barked.

Once out and safely in the front garden Charlie did a recce. Head down nose to the ground, he was in his element. He did the necessary, marking the boundary several times. Every time Bob called his name and the dog looked up he was praised and rewarded by a tiny titbit. Bob had opened the front door, whistling for the dog to follow. Charlie obliged, curious to see what his new home looked like.

He had liked the kitchen. It had a laminate floor. It looked like oak. Nice. Warm, unlike the cold slate one in Mrs Jenkins' new kitchen. A scatter rug. Chewable if he got bored? There was a small table with a bag of food on it. Round the table were four chairs. Charlie thought everything you would expect to find in a kitchen. Cupboards, cooker, fridge/freezer. What next? He looked round to see Bob opening the door of a large cupboard. From it came a dish for food and a stainless steel water bowl which Bob rinsed, and filled. He put both on the floor.

Now, before we go any further, some of you who haven't read Charlie's first adventure will be wondering who Mr. and Mrs Jenkins were. They owned the farm in Pembrokeshire where Charlie and his brothers and sister had been born. Charlie had lived there before being bought by Bob.

Bob rummaged in the bag again , and took out a casserole dish. Charlie smelled chicken. He loved casseroles. His favourite was beef, but he liked chicken too! ' What have we got here Charlie? At least it will do me until tomorrow'. Charlie sat head on one side and gazed at Bob. His bright eyes following him as the man who had put a portion of the food on a plate, opened the door of the microwave and set the timer to reheat.

Charlie gazed at his dish. Empty.   Maybe this was the first course. The microwave pinged. Charlie looked up in hope but was bitterly disappointed when he realised casserole was not for him. He whined. Bob laughed at the expression on the dog's face . Food shopping tomorrow, promise. Maybe some of the casserole, we'll see.

Food over it had been time to explore. Bob opened the kitchen door revealing a small hall, with stairs to the left. In front across the hall was another door. Charlie realized there were two halves to this. The upper one lay flat against the wall. The lower portion had a latch and it was this that Bob lifted before going into the room.

'Nice' was Charlie's first reaction, followed by 'cosy.' A soft oatmeal carpet covered the floor. In front of Charlie was a fireplace with a mantelpiece surrounding it. He could see various pictures of dogs. Some were with people. He would have a closer look later. In front of the fireplace was a settee. Charlie sniffed this. Just like my old one that Mrs Jenkins had thrown out he thought.

Somehow I don't think Mrs Jenkins would have agreed. This one was beige, almost new and of soft leather. The old one the farmer's wife had thrown away had seen better days and was of material, and although Charlie had loved its smells Mrs Jenkins hadn't!

To each side of the settee was an easy chair. On the far wall, to the left of the fireplace, was a large glass fronted mahogany bookcase. It was full of books. No space anywhere. There were even a few books on the floor. Near one of the easy chairs was a small round table.

Charlie yawned and looked round the room again. He imagined what it would feel like on a cold rainy night, curled up on the settee. He sighed. Bob glanced down interpreting the dog's sighs. Charlie would have to learn that his place was in his bed or on the carpet, not the settee. However, the best laid plans!

Man and dog settled down, Bob on the settee, Charlie on the carpet. From his pocket Bob took out his phone and made several calls, one to the vet, the other to the microchip company. Apart from the long case clock ticking in the hall all was quiet. Bob stroked the dog's head gently with one hand whilst answering his phone with the other.

Charlie was feeling sleepy. With a tum full of food and a warm carpet to lie on he relaxed, head on paws and eyes closed. He began to dream. He was back on the farm saying goodbye to his mum and dad, Mr. and Mrs Jenkins, and the children, Richard and Alys. And Rosie of course. He felt his spirit guide nearby, the outline was stronger now. He wondered why?

Bob was also feeling comfortable and sleepy. Both dozed. The ringing of the phone woke them up. Charlie opened one eye then closed it again. Bob looked round then realised while he had been sleeping Charlie had got up on the settee and had snuggled down at his side. First lesson Bob thought to himself.

He stood up. 'Charlie' he called. The dog, eyes open, lifted his head, looked at the man but didn't move. 'Charlie' Bob called again using a coaxing voice as he tapped his leg. Man and dog looked at each other. Neither wanted to give way. Bob went into the kitchen and brought Charlie's lead back with him. He clipped it on. 'Charlie' he said for the third time, giving a gentle tug on the lead as he spoke. This time Charlie jumped down and was suitably rewarded. However, at the back of his mind was a thought!

CHAPTER THREE

It was on the second day in his new home, that he had met Megan. That was the day of the accident of course. However, at the time he hadn't known that!

He had been having breakfast wondering where the dog he could smell was hiding and food over had begun to search, sniffing everywhere. There was a dog basket, but no dog!

Bob saw the dog sniffing. 'It's Megan's' he said as Charlie looked up enquiringly. 'No, she's not here right now but she normally lives here and you'll be meeting her later. His head on one side as if he understood; Charlie gazed at Bob who laughed.

'She's at my sister Jean's. Megan's a retriever, not so young now, but she still loves the odd bit of Search and Rescue work. I'm hoping she'll be able to teach you a thing or two.' Bob carried on talking to Charlie just as he had always done to his dogs. 'We'll go and fetch her then do a shop. You'll need a bed of your own for here, and a snuggly round fluffy one for the lounge. Megan doesn't like them and prefers the carpet. I gave her old one away, but I have a feeling you'll love one. We'll see.'

No sooner had the car stopped outside his sister's house then the front door burst open and out came Alex and Holly, 'Where is he?' they demanded. 'Hang on just a minute, how about Hi Uncle Bob nice to see you.' They all laughed. Jean came out and Megan with her.

'Let's do this outside on the green. It's neutral ground for both of them.' As he spoke Bob opened the car door picking up the dog's lead before calling to Charlie to come. The dog jumped out looking round eagerly. Alex and Holly made a fuss of Charlie and laughed as he licked them in turn. 'Now let's see how the dogs get on' Bob said. Both dogs stared at each other then cautiously approached and did the normal rear end sniffing etc. Megan was relaxed. So was Charlie. No threat there.

In Jean's garden both dogs were now off their leads but were carefully watched by everyone. Charlie offered a play bow and Megan was happy to play for a few minutes. After that she took no notice of Charlie though he bounced round her barking as if to say more, more, more. He'd have another try later he thought. She seemed gentle and very obedient and sensible.

Charlie wasn't sure he liked sensible or obedient come to that, especially if the latter clashed with what he wanted to do! He liked the children though. They reminded him a little of the twins, though they didn't smell the same. What else?

Well Alex, was the taller of the two, by something called 'a head'. This was the word he had heard Mrs Jenkins use when she had measured the twins. The boy was dressed in grey trousers, had a blue sweatshirt with writing on, and wore lace up trainers. He had fair hair, as did his sister and their mum. Cool!

Alex smelled of the outdoors and his hands were gentle. Holly was slightly shorter, and wore her hair in plaits. She had an impish grin on her face, and her hands were soft and light as they stroked Charlie. Both children smelled good to him as did their mum Jean, who had a soft, kind voice. They all talked to him as they made a fuss of him and Megan. 'Can't leave you out can we Megan?' said Jean, the children's mum who happened, just happened, to have, treats in her pocket. In Charlie's book that's what counted. Like many dogs he wasn't all that keen on hugs so was pleased when after a few pats no hugs were forthcoming. **Any idea why many dogs don't like to be hugged?**

'Where are you off to now?' Jean asked. 'Farmers Market for veggies, Then the Pet Shop. I need a harness for Charlie . After that, a quick trip to the butcher, then home.' Bob didn't want to flood Charlie with too many new things at once, but thought he might take the dog with him to the market.

CHAPTER FOUR

Just after eight am and the stallholders at the Farmers' Market had already set up their stands. Charlie breathed in the smells. Vegetables; cheese; bread; cakes; meat, dog biscuits? Yes, homemade dog biscuits. Jams and marmalade and other things too.

Walking from stall to stall Charlie had behaved well, though a few people had remarked on his appearance. The stall selling bread and cakes was busy, but Bob managed to get his favourite cake, a ca----l eclair.

Charlie joined Megan in the car and Bob set off to the pet shop. He took Charlie in and found a harness. It was adjustable, just the thing. Back in the car the dog settled down and curled up to Megan. Now to the butchers.

'Hi Bob.' Mr. Blockwell's smiling face greeted him. 'What can I do for you?

'First of all marrow bones, two if you've got them. I'm low on bone broth. Need to do a new batch'.

The butcher looked at him. 'I reckon that means a new dog. Am I right?' Bob laughed. 'He's outside in the car. His name's Charlie. He's a seven month old Border Collie with a remarkable ability. I'm hoping we can channel that energy so that in the end he becomes a search and rescue dog.'

Bob quickly told the story about Charlie and how he found Rosie. 'My word' said Mr. Blackwell. 'Reckon you might have something special there.' Bob nodded.

'Anything else?'

'Yes, 1 lb of liver. I've a liver cake to make for the dogs' he added, as one of the customers looked up enquiringly. 'You know how Megan loves pieces as a reward and I hope Charlie will be the same. Oh and some mince. You know how Megan likes her mince and garlic.' There was laughter in the shop and joking and Bob laughed as he was teased. 'You and your dogs' said one. 'Why don't you give em an all in one, it's so much easier?'

'Maybe but I promised his breeders I would feed him properly, and where possible keep to what they have done. Which means a raw diet with extras, like vegetables and some fruit, and a good pro-biotic etc. That's the way I have always fed though others may disagree.'

'That it then?' said Mr. Blockwell? Bob hesitated. He really fancied steak, and onions, with chips, gravy and masses of veggies. It wasn't really an extravagance. After all any extra veggies the dogs would have mixed in with their own food later. His mouth was watering at the thought of his meal that night. Bet you have something that is your favourite. So you will know exactly what Bob was feeling as he stood there in the shop. He could almost see the food on the table. Just this once, he told himself. 'Steak' he said pointing to one piece in the middle of two others.

'Right, let's see this wonder dog of yours then'. The burly butcher walked out with him to the car.

CHAPTER FIVE

Of course , if you've read Charlie to the Rescue' you've probably guessed what comes next. The butcher stared at Charlie. 'Blimey Bob he's got odd eyes, and one ear stands up and the other is flat against his head!'

Bob smiled. 'Really?' He laughed. ' That alone makes him special. At first Charlie had tensed up. He'd heard those words and that tone of voice before. Would he once again even in a new home be laughed at and found wanting. But his heart filled with joy at Bob's words and the love he felt in his voice. Like young Rosie Bob really did love him for himself and not how he looked, though really there was nothing wrong with his looks was there? We are all different, so why not dogs?

Had Charlie listened to the end of the conversation he would have heard the butcher say that a long time ago his granddad had a dog just like Charlie. He had reckoned it was the most intelligent dog he had ever owned.

Charlie wasn't listening though so didn't hear it but vowed there and then that he would try to do his utmost to please Bob. How hard could that be, he asked himself? Hmm! Bob was just going home when he saw the list he had made on the front seat. What had he forgotten to get? Whatever it was it would have to wait for another day. He needed to get both dogs settled. This was the most important thing. Thank goodness he had a few days in hand before starting a new job.   Jean was popping in at lunch time so Charlie could get used to her being there.

At home Bob went through his list.   Spare covers for the dog bed.   He'd got one for Megan but knew Charlie with his thick coat would need more than one. Dog rescue shop or store? He might find something in the charity shop but then maybe not.

Yes a new Kong was definitely needed. The rubber of Megan's old one was perished. He'd also read somewhere, though he couldn't remember where, someone saying to give your new addition toys of its own. Sensible he had thought, after all the other would feel the new dog was getting all the current one's toys.   He wondered how Charlie would react to toys and the interactive games he had bought for Megan. She'd not shown much interest in them, so he'd put them away, but Charlie now

Charlie was totally different. So, maybe!
He stood watching Charlie and Megan in the garden. He was on his way back to the kitchen to make a drink when he heard the phone ring.   Convinced the dogs were safe he went to answer the phone, and we know that's when disaster struck.

Back home after the trip to the vets with the dogs safely in the kitchen, Bob went to make himself a drink.   The caramel éclair was still there waiting, just waiting to be eaten!   This was his favourite but he really didn't feel like it now. Tea in hand, he thought about ringing The Jenkins. To be honest he wasn't sure what to say. If he rang and told them about Charlie would they think he had been careless? But not to be honest was not in his nature and he felt he owed it to them to be upfront.   Courage he thought! Now to ring, no more putting off that phone call.

Mrs Jenkins answered. 'Well isn't that like Charlie' she said. 'He acts first then thinks afterwards'. To his apology she told him accidents did happen and that maybe after this Charlie would begin to listen and be responsible.' She ended by thanking him for ringing adding 'take care of yourselves and keep in touch.' After the call ended Bob felt a great sense of relief. He knew he had done the right thing in 'phoning'. Wasn't he always telling his sister's two children, Alex and Holly, as did their parents, that honesty was the best policy.

He remembered the time when as children he and his sister Jean had broken one of their mum's favourite vases. They had hidden the pieces. However, in the end they had owned up because not saying anything was worse. Their mum had hugged them saying how much she loved them for being honest. Now time for that cuppa and the eclair.

He had just taken the milk out of the fridge when his mobile rang. It was a colleague from Search and Rescue. Chris. Bob listened then said' yes Charlie was very lucky. He and Megan had met up earlier and all was well. He's still sore of course. I hate to think what would have happened if those cars were going faster than they were. I'm going to rest him up for a few days but maybe we can all meet up after that. I'll give you a ring.'

Now, where had he put those interactive puzzles. Loft or garage? He remembered the talk a vet/ behaviourist had given the team. These puzzles help a dog to think and use its brain trying to work out how to get the treats inside them.

A dog needed to be tired out both physically and mentally. What else had the behaviourist said? It was slowly coming back to him. He'd been doing things for Megan so long now most things were automatic. That's right. Now he remembered - the importance of chewing, tearing and ripping Not clothes of course, but using teeth, and jaws, and energy in getting its food.

Why do you think this is important?

Thinking of puzzles reminded him of the one Chris used with her dog Sasha. She'd got the idea she explained after watching a tv programme or was it a YouTube video? He couldn't remember.

It showed a large dog who had successfully worked out how to retrieve treats from plastic bottles suspended on a bar across a wooden frame. The dog had to work out the right speed for the bottles to spin and drop out the treats. Ingenious! Chris's friend had made something similar to the one on the programme.

Idly Bob wondered how long it would take Charlie to work out the speed needed for the bottles to spin and the treats drop out. He knew the dog was bright and needed to be mentally challenged. He hoped he had been right to think that once the dog was doing obedience work and learning the skills required of a search and rescue dog he'd forget about wanting to be off exploring. Then, hopefully no more straying and escaping to find all those smells he loved. Least that's what he was hoping! That was the plan!

Tomorrow or perhaps the day after, he would start some obedience training with Charlie. He knew Charlie had potential and guessed there would be times the dog would test him to the limit.

First in the kitchen he would practise the 'look' signal. Call the dog's name, When he looked up put your finger to your nose (say 'look') then when the dog's attention was on you give him a treat. Charlie looked up as Bob called his name. He got up stiffly from his basket. Bob offered him a treat, praising him as he did. Once was enough for now.

CHAPTER SIX

The following day it rained heavily. No point in trying to train outdoors in this especially with a young dog. Although he was able to do the 'look at me' signal again followed quickly by reward. Great way to distract a dog and get it to focus on the handler. Useful too. Right, indoor training, with a different form of mental and physical stimulation. Interactive puzzles.

He looked out of the window again later. Still raining. Just the sort of day to be by the fire in the warmth and comfort, work permitting. He thanked his lucky stars once again that the owner of the cottage he was renting had put in a downstairs shower when he modernized.

At times when he and Megan had come back exhausted and wet after a search out call it was wonderful just to step into the shower. Wash and dry her properly, then take a shower himself, flinging his dirty clothes into the washer.

Thinking about showering and drying the dogs he remembered something else to add to his list. A good quality dog drying coat for Charlie. He had seen some in the pet shop. He'd glanced at them but done no more. The quality wasn't that good and to work properly coats had to be both the right fit and quality. Cheap never lasted. He'd wait for the sales then order on line. A while later he glanced out of the window. Was it his imagination or was the rain letting up slightly? It was, so change of plan. A short walk just part way down the lane with a little training thrown in was good.

Charlie had done well. Watching then following what Megan did. He had actually come each time when called, The dog's long line for the most part was loose. Several short sessions were far better than a long one. Stop before the dog became bored. Make things fun. Bob noticed that Charlie didn't seem to mind the rain which was good. Just as well, as he would need to be able to work in all weathers and happily too.

Training over, dogs dried and back in the warmth, now to start the bone broth off and the liver cake. Bob found the slow cooker, put in the marrow bones, added garlic, and then water, and last of all the secret ingredient. One hour on high, then twenty-four hours on low, etc. Although he checked the recipe again it was one he knew by heart. It didn't hurt to check though. Other ingredients to follow after cooking time.

His sister had saved quite a few plastic topped containers so when the broth was cold and the fat skimmed off it could be put into these and then into the freezer. From what he remembered there would be a good three weeks' supply. Slow cooker on, now for the liver cake. He laughed to himself. How much more domesticated could he be?

Jean had given her brother her old mixer when she bought a new one so out it came from the cupboard. No need to weigh the liver he had one lb exactly. Flour measured out, eggs on the side ready to be added, as was water, he lined two sponge tins, inherited from his mum, then carefully reading the recipe again put the first ingredients into the blender. When everything had been mixed and divided between the tins he checked the oven temperature before putting the prepared liver cake in to cook. Mustn't forget the timer!

Tea time. After heating up some of the casserole for himself Bob fed the dogs the remains then said 'let's go', calling for the dogs to go outside and do the necessary.

He saved the command 'come' when he needed Megan and Charlie to come to him. The combination of signal and word was one he had perfected over the years. It was now second nature to him. Cleaning up after them Bob headed back to the house and the warmth. In the lounge Megan settled down on the carpet. She had a touch of arthritis as many older dogs do but her medication helped and here on the soft carpet she was fine.

Charlie eventually settled into the round fluffy bed Jean and the children had bought him as a present. However, he kept eyeing the settee longingly. It was so much nicer. He was suddenly aware his spirit guide or ancestor some would say was near. He saw his vague outline. Charlie hadn't thought about him for several days, not since the time of the accident. Why was he here now?

Man and dogs dozed. The rain had started again. Bob could hear it beating against the windows but in the room all was snug and cosy. Megan wasn't thinking of anything in particular. She thought she would get used to Charlie. True he was bouncy and she really didn't do bouncy, but he was young and good natured and Bob, Jean and the children liked him and as she said to herself that's what's important.
Bob woke suddenly. Megan was whining slightly. He looked at her. She had raised her head and was staring intently at something in the corner of the room. He looked but there was nothing. At least nothing he could see. Curious. It was not like her to whine for no reason. He looked at her again. Whatever she saw didn't bother her and after a few minutes and a quick

look at Charlie Megan lowered her head, sighed, and went to sleep, head on paws.

She can see him Charlie thought in surprise. He wondered if he had come to talk to Megan, but no the shadow dog was quiet. He was waiting until the time was right to approach Charlie. He knew the man was good and kind and that Charlie had been lucky. Charlie's star might still be small but it was glowing, a sure sign his heart was in the right place.

He had recently visited another dog where conditions were very different, and the dog's star had almost vanished. He needed to let Charlie know how other dogs lived so he waited patiently for the right moment before whispering in his ears.

Charlie took it all in, his large ears twitching. The shadow dog, Charlie thought of him more and more often now as his spirit guide , warned that sometimes those who owned dogs didn't always do the right thing by them. Occasionally it was because people didn't realise. At times it was because people did not care. Sometimes because of this a dog lost heart and his character could alter.

'Charlie, as you get older you may be able to tell when people are good or not so good by their smell. I did' he said. 'Not just their own smell but the smells that hang round them. Smells from the animals they have kept. Sometimes smells that detect their people, or even other dogs, may not be in the best of health.'

Charlie didn't understand all he was being told but he knew that his spirit guide had to be right. He usually was. 'Don't question what your nose tells you' were the last words Charlie heard, plus remember to listen,' before he fell asleep.

CHAPTER SEVEN

The next day was glorious. After the rain everything smelled fresh. The sun shone and the weather forecast was good. The colours of the leaves on the trees were wonderful. Time to go somewhere different Bob thought. Let's see what he makes of the forestry trail.

So with a backpack, flask of tea, an apple, and water for the dogs and of course doggy poo bags, he set off. Out of the car, initially on a long line, Charlie barked excitedly and head down began to sniff. Megan walked down the two section mobile ramp attached to the boot of the car. She could have jumped down bur Bob didn't want her landing and possibly worsening the arthritis so he had bought the ramp. It was ideal.

Megan knew this place of old and was looking forward to a leisurely stroll. The nearby forestry path was quiet. Charlie kept dashing off to left and right of the path but came back every time when called, and on the whole the long line remained slack. A good sign. Bob was feeling delighted. All was going well. He'd cracked it. Really! He took the line off.

Charlie, head down, was sniffing it seemed at every blade of grass, every leaf. Don't want to miss anything he thought. A few times Bob had gently thrown a small rubber ball for Charlie. The dog had run after it before bringing it back, so it could be thrown again. His bright eyes were alight with happiness and as he waited for Bob to throw the ball again the dog barked impatiently. Come on he seemed to say.

The first difficulty arose when suddenly the smell hit him. The one he had encountered when he first arrived at his new home. He had forgotten it for a while but here it was again. It wasn't a true countryside smell. It wasn't, yet it was. He stood, looking around, ears alert trying to sense where it was coming from.

Bob's comment 'Charlie come' made him hesitate. He wanted to come back, he really did, but! In the end the call of the scent was too much to bear so he tore off. He was deaf to Bob's call and Megan's bark. Half an hour had gone by and although Bob had repeatedly called Charlie the dog had not returned.

Time for Megan to do her stuff. She sat patiently looking up, waiting for the command. 'Find him girl'. She had been enjoying herself and here was Charlie spoiling everything by not listening and doing his own thing. It was high time he learned!

Fifteen minutes later and no sign of either dog. Bob was worried. Then he heard Megan bark somewhere up ahead. He turned the corner and running towards him was Megan, but no Charlie. She barked again then turned and went back up the track, Bob following. She veered off the track through bushes then stopped and barked again.

It was as he was running to catch up with her that he saw Charlie. The dog was stuck. Well and truly stuck, caught in brambles. Beyond the brambles there was fencing across the path with a small gap in it. Charlie had obviously thought he could scramble through this. He was wrong. How on earth was Bob going to get him out?

He carefully walked towards the dog keeping his voice low.
He didn't want to frighten him and cause him to struggle and
enmesh himself even further in the brambles. He needed help
and help fast. Chris was probably the nearest. But would she be
home, working?

No answer from her mobile, but he left a message, giving her
the co-ordinates from the map app on his phone. If only he
had thought to put in a large pair of scissors, but he hadn't
thought he'd need them. He looked again in his pack and saw a
small pair. OK for cutting a bandage but no good for what was
needed today.

His phone rang. It was Chris. Bob explained the position and
repeated the co-ordinates. As luck would have it she had just
come in. 'Give me five minutes to change and make a drink
then I'm on my way. Twenty minutes and he was still waiting.
No sign of Chris. It was then he heard the sound and coming
towards them was a battered old truck. He couldn't see the
figure at the wheel.

It certainly wasn't Chris, nor was it her truck. The driver
opened the door and jumped down. It was a man in old jeans
with a forestry commission logo on his shirt. Bob recognised
Ewan, Chris's brother. The family worked the smallholding in
the next valley, had done so for generations and Ewan, who had
recently left college, had been taken on as a trainee with the
local Forestry Commission. No one knew the land and paths
round here better than Ewan; all the short cuts too.
'Trust you' were his first words, as he looked at Charlie. 'Knew
it had to be the dog when Chris rang to say you were in trouble.
That dog's accident prone. I'd get rid of him if I were you. He's
more trouble than he's worth.' He wasn't but Bob unwilling to
be drawn into an argument defending Charlie just shrugged his
shoulders, commenting 'he's certainly a one off. I'll give you

that?' He knew in his heart of hearts that sometimes difficult dogs were actually the brightest and when young would test all the boundaries.

Big shearing scissors in his hand Ewan commented 'can't save all his coat I'm afraid, and he'll look a little like a shorn lamb but at least we can get him out. You'll owe me big time though. A few beers at the week-end should do it' he continued as he snipped away. At last Charlie was free.

Back at home Charlie felt completely humiliated. He had stood meekly while parts of his coat were being cut off. Megan had turned her back on him in disgust, and as for Bob! All he said was 'Oh Charlie' but his voice was so sad, despondent you might say, that Charlie hung his head. Showered now and dried he looked a scruff. Bob tidied the dog up, fed him and Megan then making himself a drink and something to eat went through into the small sitting room. He rang his sister, who after laughing at Charlie's predicament said she would be over in the morning and would tidy the dog up. Jean had often helped trim Megan, her experience as a hairdresser standing her in good stead. For competitions Megan always looked magnificent.

CHAPTER EIGHT

Jean put the phone down and wondered. She'd been looking at job adverts but nothing appealed. Now the children were older perhaps she could find a part time job; one that fitted in with school hours? But what? She'd trained as a hairdresser and occasionally did people's hair at home . She had started to trim Megan as a dare really, after the bitch had come back from a session at a groomers looking less than perfect. She had bet Bob she could do as good a job if not better. She'd won the bet and had been grooming her ever since. Even kept her scissors and grooming kit etc in a special box. First there was Megan, now Charlie who needed a makeover! It was as she was thinking this that an idea popped into her mind. How about doing a dog grooming course and working from home? Perhaps she could turn the garage into a grooming parlour? That way she'd still be at home but could also earn some money. It all helped especially with Alex and Holly forever needing things. Must ask Stewart what he thinks she thought, thinking of her husband who worked as a manager in a local supermarket.

At Bob's Charlie sat at his feet looking up at him, and licking his hand. With a sigh Bob absently stroked the dog's head. Could have been worse he thought. Megan had found him and both dogs were safe. Later that night as he went to sleep he thought about a saying his dad had often used – tomorrow's another day. Megan snored softly in her bed uttering little sounds from time to time. Charlie lay awake. He had really wanted to please Bob and he had tried, really he had, but something had come over him.

'Charlie' came the soft word. Charlie cautiously opened one eye, then closed it again. He didn't want to see his spirit guide, especially now. He knew a talking to was on the cards and he didn't want that although he knew he deserved it.

When his name was called a second time Charlie heaved a sigh and looked up. There was sadness in the other dog's eyes. Charlie's heart sank. He felt so ashamed. He needed to do better. This was followed by the fact that he didn't want to be sent away. He loved Bob and Megan too. What if Bob listened to Ewan and sold him. Where would he go? Charlie couldn't bear that thought. Never see all those he loved. His heart would break. He was sure of that.

'You know what I'm going to say don't you?' Charlie nodded. 'I know you have it in you to do yourself and those who love you proud. You've learned a hard lesson today. What would have happened if out on a mission you went dashing off just because you wanted to follow a smell you hadn't come across before?'

'Today you weren't searching for anyone, but imagine you had been. When you are working you must concentrate. No good finding the casualty then dashing off to go after a rabbit or something. That way not only will you fail any test but you will never make a search and rescue dog. Bob needs to be able to trust and depend on you. If Megan hadn't been with him and found you just think what the outcome would have been. That's all I have to say.'

However, just before he faded away Charlie thought he saw him smile and say that he knew what it was like as he too had been young once. Megan was still asleep and Charlie knew she had been tired searching for him. Sighing, he curled himself up into a tight ball, nose to tail, and eventually went to sleep.

The next day when Bob returned from work it was to see a transformed Charlie. True one side of his coat was slightly shorter but unless you looked at both sides together you would hardly notice. He hugged his sister and thanked her again for the great job she had done. 'No, I insist' he said as she refused to take any money. 'You have done me a real favour and a professional groomer would have charged far more, plus the story would have been round the village in no time.'

Jean eyed the delicious coffee and walnut cake. If Bob's favorite was a caramel éclair, hers was coffee and walnut cake. 'Well, I will stay for a quick cuppa and a slice of that delicious looking cake then I must be off as I have tea to prepare. Sure you don't want to come? It's spag bol, so there's plenty of it.' Bob shook his head. 'No thanks. After tea Charlie and I are going to do a little more training on his recall. Wish me luck.' She did.

For the next month Charlie was on his best behaviour. Alex and Holly came to take out both dogs on short walks after school, as Bob always took them out before going to work. He would pop in at lunch time too if his sister couldn't get there.

There were occasional arguments between Alex and Holy as to who should have Charlie and who should have Megan, but brothers and sisters often have disagreements. However, they never lasted long. In the end they agreed each would take turns. So if Holly took Charlie out, she would have Megan on the way back.

CHAPTER NINE

Charlie's training was going well. It was now several months down the line and although there had been a few hiccups these had been sorted out. He'd met the other dogs and passed his puppy acceptance into the team test; obedience, and then stock test. The last one was carried out annually, whichever branch of SARDA you were with. The puppy test looked at play drive, willingness to explore, natural ability, sociability etc.

The dog rescue team usually met up on the Saturday morning for a practise. The volunteers discussed the programme for the day. Bob was teamed with Chris She was their dogsbody. He was hers. Later it was the turn of one or two of the others.

Stage 1 – Indication Test. This was to see if the dog had a reliable indication. Yes, there was no doubt about it. Charlie certainly had that. Bob beamed with delight. He felt like a child at school winning a prize and wanted everyone to see and say well done. Each time Chris hid Charlie found her and indicated. He dashed back to Bob tongue hanging out and then went back to her, going between the two. 'Good boy Charlie'. Bob threw him the ball praising the dog for all he was worth. The ball was Charlie's reward for doing well. The next few times the dogsbody was further away. After that she was even further away.

Each time Charlie sat waiting for Bob's command. The dog was like a coiled spring – raring to go. His tail flicking backwards and forwards. His eyes were bright and alert. He was having a wonderful time . No sooner had Bob released him then off he went.

At the end of their session and what was hard work the dogs were dried off, fed and watered then left to rest on vetbeds in their owner's cars. Warm and comfortable. The volunteers had a twenty minute break. Time for a hot drink and a sandwich, before it was the turn of the older dogs. Not all volunteers were there but even so another few hours passed before the coordinator called it a day.

Bob looked at Charlie quietly snoozing in the car and remembered the time Megan was a novice dog and had first qualified. Assessments were yearly. Now she was a veteran so to speak, though fully graded dog was the correct term, she was assessed every three years. How different in temperament were his two dogs. Megan had always been obedient even when young, whereas Charlie!

They were two different breeds of course, bred to do different jobs of work, so why on earth should they respond in exactly the same way? He thought of his sister Jean. Alex and Holly were about 5 or 6 he remembered and had badgered Jean and Stewart for a puppy for a long time. In the end their parents had agreed. One Sunday afternoon they had taken them to visit a friend whose bitch had recently had a litter of puppies. It was a mistake! They should have gone first, talked about it then if they were agreed taken the children to look.

As soon as the children saw the puppies that was it. Jean wasn't sure but Stewart assured her it would be all right. How much trouble would it be to bring up a puppy? He was called Teddy, was from a working strain and even with Jean taking him to classes the dog needed more mental stimulation than she could give. Walks weren't enough. He had started to destroy things through boredom, and learned how to open cupboards and the washing machine.

Coming in from shopping one afternoon Jean had found tins of food and packets of pasta and rice ripped open, the contents scattered all over the kitchen floor. Enough was enough. Fortunately the washing machine had been empty but if it hadn't!

Talking to Stewart that evening they both agreed Teddy needed something to do. He needed to work. After all that's what he was bred to do. So, she had asked the vet if he knew of someone looking for a youngster. 'He is very bright but needs to work.' The vet didn't but said that he would ask around. To keep Teddy out of the cupboards Stewart had installed a child lock, adding one to the fridge door too – to be on the safe side.

Frustrated from enjoying himself Teddy then found something else to do. He started gnawing the wood handles of the kitchen drawers. It was the vet who saved the situation. He had been called out to a client, whose brother lived near Sandringham in Norfolk. His brother was a gamekeeper and was looking for a new dog. In the end it all worked out perfectly. Jean was sad to see Teddy go and the children were upset.

Before they said goodbye to him Jean and Stewart had sat down with Alex and Holly and discussed Teddy and the fact that he was growing older and was obviously unhappy as he didn't have enough to do. 'Imagine how bored you would be if we didn't go out and do different things, and we were just stuck in the house except for a few walks.' Stewart continued 'we have had a word with the vet and he agrees that Teddy is very bright and needs to be doing more. It is hard I know as we all love Teddy but we have to think what is best for him don't we?'

In his new home Teddy thrived. No more boredom. No more chewing and destroying things. Now he had to work and use his brain. He used up so much energy at the end of the day he was exhausted, but it felt good. The family had decided no more dogs for them. However, they were lucky as there was Uncle Bob and Megan. So Megan became a real family dog, sharing her life with them all. It had worked out well.

Bob was a self-employed joiner. He had passed his apprenticeship with a firm that made bespoke kitchen furniture etc, and had recently set up on his own. He was recommended by the firm concerned as his work was excellent. He was a real craftsman. Sometimes he had to travel a distance to install a kitchen or fit an expensive staircase etc and might take a few days' holiday at the same time. Megan loved her own little holidays when she stayed with her extended family. She was looked after as if she were their own. In a way she was wasn't she?

Jean now thought of Charlie and wondered how he was doing. She hoped for Bob' sake the dog would learn to adjust. That he was intelligent she knew beyond any doubt. Watching a dog training programme on the tv she remembered the comment made to the effect that a search and rescue dog needed to be intelligently disobedient. Well, that certainly fitted Charlie. At home Megan and Charlie were talking about their day as dogs do. Charlie was excitedly filling her in with all the details. At first she listened but after a while it became a little boring. After all she was used to this but she could understand Charlie being excited.

She tactfully tried to tell him a few things but as usual Charlie wasn't really listening. However, once settled for the night he began to think about her words and caution. After all he didn't

want the other dogs to think he was big headed, did he?   That
would never do.

Not all the dogs are friendly Megan had said. They don't all
want to share things.   She paused. There is one large dog,
called Dusty.   He wasn't there today. Be very careful of him.
He is not all friendly. He is great at finding casualties but! He
is an ex police dog, and had to leave through ill health.   He
loves his handler but most of the other dogs are slightly scared
of him.

CHAPTER TEN

Looking at his dogs now in the kitchen Bob realized how much Charlie had grown, had filled out. Had matured. Well, he smiled to himself, at least physically. As to mentally? True he hadn't been as 'in your face' (as Holly would say) lately, but he was still unpredictable at times. He was a challenge, yet Bob could see something in Charlie no one else could.

At a recent meeting all the volunteers had listened to reports which had come in from various sectors. There was one which had made them smile, though it had meant they had been called out for nothing. However, a call was a call and they always went.

There'd been a call to the police by friends of two walkers, a couple, who had failed to meet the party at the arranged rendezvous. The Police contacted Search and Rescue. They listened to the information and got ready to search. However within 10 minutes of being called there was good news. Apparently ,as the weather looked bad, the two walkers had abandoned their walk without telling anyone, They had decided to go to the nearest pub. Unfortunately, they had forgotten the meet up time and consequently turned up late. Red faces all round, and abject apologies. **Sometimes there would be the odd situation like this**.

The walkers had been extremely apologetic. Their friends were less forgiving! All made donations to Search and Rescue, and the walkers concerned promised never again to do something so thoughtless.

Reports were varied. One call had been about someone who was at high risk but had fortunately been found safe and well. The dog had located her. Then a call where a local resident had telephoned 999 as she was concerned about two people believed to be stuck up a nearby mountain. A local member of the nearby rescue team went out to look but was unable to find anyone either in distress or requiring help. Although it was registered as a false alarm, it had been a call made with good intentions. Other call outs varied from finding walkers badly injured or in need of urgent medical attention, to those who had sprained ankles and could be helped back to base, and others who were lost due to changes in the weather.

One afternoon a call had been received. There were two women walkers plus their large somewhat elderly dog. The women seemed all right but part way towards the summit their dog had suddenly sat down and refused to move any further. Help was needed. It turned out the dogs' paws were cracked and blistered and the dog had to be stretchered down the mountain and taken to a vet for treatment.

Over the next four months or so Charlie's training continued. He was becoming more obedient though he still had his moments. He was growing now in strength and ability.

The test for Stage 2 was coming up soon. Would he pass it? Bob was nervous. Not all dogs managed it. This one involved 2 tests where the dog had to search for multiple bodies, spaced out in different parts of a certain agreed area.

Only the co-ordinator and the dogsbodies knew the hiding places and how many bodies the dog had to find. Had he done enough with Charlie? Was it too soon to test him? Perhaps he should have waited. He knew that some of the dogs had located say two of the three bodies yet failed to find the third. That was upsetting for them. Without being told the dogs knew they had failed.

This test was hard as the dogs were deliberately confused by different scents. The co-ordinator said nothing when dogs and handlers returned from their test. Only at the end were the results given.

The handlers gathered round the co-ordinator as the results were read out. Charlie had passed. Bob felt such a feeling of pride and relief. Yet sorry for those whose dogs had failed to locate say a third body.

CHAPTER ELEVEN

It was a warm and sunny day. Bob was trimming his elderly neighbour's hedge, a little at a time, and later on would mow the lawn. As it was such a glorious day and there was plenty of shade he decided to take the dogs with him. Another session and the hedge should be finished. Maybe after a cuppa he would take the dogs for a nice long walk .

On the lawn, on his back, paws up, Charlie was playing with a small piece of wood he had found. Bob checked it carefully. Safe he thought. Megan was soaking up the sun eyes closed. Charlie was bored. He didn't like all this lying about doing nothing. He dropped the wood, got up and stretched. What to do next. It was when he was bored he often found trouble. He'd said to Megan that he never looked for trouble, but somehow it always managed to find him. She hadn't looked convinced. Wonder why? What do you think?

Nice smelling flowers he thought. He wandered a little further exploring the rose bushes. It was then he found it. There was wire stretched between the rose bushes and the back wall.

Trouble was that there was a tiny gap near the bottom of the wire. It was the tiniest of spaces but Charlie had spotted it. He saw that the wire was being held in place by a small piece of what was now rotten wood. Maybe the wire had sagged a little over the years, but there it was. It was an invitation too good to miss. Bob had never thought to check behind the bushes to make sure everything was safe. Why would he? 'I'll remember this' Charlie thought.

Now during Bob's second hedge trimming visit Charlie had perfected his plan. He wasn't going to share it with Megan, as he didn't think she would be interested.

'Charlie' said his spirit ancestor one night. 'Do you really think this scheme of yours is a good idea? Charlie had pretended to be asleep. He didn't want anything to stop him from carrying out his plan.

The first time Charlie had been very careful to keep an eye on Bob as the dog began to lean against the wire. If he could manage to stretch the wire one of the wood posts would come out and he could scramble free. This was going to take careful planning. He must not be caught.

Each time Charlie saw Bob begin to turn he came out of the bushes and sauntered back to the grass or sat lying in the sun as if he were asleep. No way was he giving the game away. Now, the hole was bigger it was time to put his plan into action. Today was the day. He was confident that Megan wouldn't give him any trouble.

He'd just look as he normally did, nose to the ground exploring. He could always say that you never knew what you might find if he didn't make it. However, he was confident he would. There was no one to give him away was there?

Earlier on Meghan had looked at him before going back to sleep. He looked round for Bob. He was at the other side of the garden clearing hedge trimmings. Charlie disappeared behind the rose bushes. Everything in place. Just a few more digs should do it. Then over the wall and freedom.

He had half his body under the wire when Megan began to bark furiously and Bob came to see what was happening. She was on her own and looking at the rose bushes. Where on earth was Charlie? She glanced at him, then back to the bushes. Just as Charlie had almost completed his escape he felt Bob's hands on his body and was jerked back. Megan a satisfied gleam in her eyes had turned traitor.

All he could do then, as he was banished indoors. was to watch from the window while Bob hammered special new pegs in the wire. Charlie wasn't sure what he felt. Part of him had been longing to escape and explore, yet there was another part of him that hadn't really wanted to go and was glad when Bob stopped him. It was a most peculiar feeling. Very unsettling. What was happening?

CHAPTER TWELVE

The next day Jean and the children turned up, with some startling news. They were probably going to be moving. Stewart her husband had applied for another job , a promotion. It was at a major grocery store and was about half an hour from Brecon, which was the nearest big town .

The opposite direction from his present post in fact but the roads were good. Most were dual carriageways. Stewart reckoned if he were offered the job and they lived locally it would be an easy commute to work.

Alex and Holly weren't so pleased. In fact they said they didn't want to go. They wanted to stay. They could stop with Uncle Bob and Megan, Alex had said and Holly had agreed.

When they realized that this was not possible Alex had stormed out of the room, banging the door behind him. They could hear him charging up to his room and the bedroom door slam. Oh dear, this was not a good start. Holly had cried then sulked, saying she was not hungry at meal times, and it was unfair she couldn't stay, as her best friend was at school and she would miss her. She'd never ever see her again she'd said. 'It's not fair'. Nothing more was said, but the not hungry spell soon ended.

Several days later when Alex and Holly had calmed down and their mum judged it was a good time to talk, their parents called a family meeting. 'Nothing is settled yet' Stewart had said. 'I haven't been offered the job. If I get the promotion we could look for a bigger house one with a garden but your mum and I wanted to prepare you for a move just in case. One of the questions I asked at the interview was about schools, and after school clubs etc ,and general sports facilities in the area, and of course a library.

The town is larger than our present one and I gather there's much more to do generally. There's The Brecon Beacons of course and as we all like walking when we can, I think we would be very happy there. So, how about we all go, explore the area and see what we think. He added that two of the managers had children at the school Alex and Holly would probably go to. 'They are the same age as you' Stewart told them. 'If I get the job they have promised to invite us round for tea so you can get to know their children before term starts'.

'What do you say?' Alex and Holly looked at each other. Maybe moving if dad got the promotion might not be as bad as they first thought. No more was said but Stewart and Jean felt at least the children appeared to be looking at things in a more positive way. Alex was still convinced none of his friends would come to visit.

'They'll come' said his mum. 'You'll have so much to tell them. Just think of the things you can all do together'. 'Oh I forgot', she added, 'I gather there's a cinema not too far away either'. As far as Alex was concerned this was the clincher. His face grew brighter.

So the family had gone to have a look at the area, just in case. There was fierce competition for the position and Stewart still had to attend several interviews. He could hardly believe his luck when he was told that the job was his. Bob was pleased for them but sad to think he wouldn't be able to see them daily anymore.

CHAPTER THIRTEEN

The farewell party was wonderful. Their parents' friends were there as were Alex and Holly's school friends. Everything you could wish for food wise was there too. Added to that there was lemonade and soft drinks for the younger children, with a variety of drinks for the adults.

Jean had prepared all the savoury food. Charlie learned later things were called canapes, and friends had brought things like trifle. There was even meringue, fruit salad, and ice cream. Nothing for him or Megan though - shame. Everyone had been given invites to visit, and, of course, Uncle Bob would be the number one guest. He would be the first one to stay in the new house.

Without his sister and her family popping in Bob's house felt very empty, even though he was busy and spent time with his colleagues. He'd arranged for someone to take the dogs out during the day. He appreciated this but missed the children and hearing what they had been up to. He wondered whether Jean had thought any more of perhaps getting a part time job or even setting up a mobile dog grooming business. She hadn't said anything and when speaking to Alex and Holly on the telephone they seemed vague.

Summer would soon be giving way to Autumn and the ferns on the hills would be turning to russet brown . They would then be ready to be cut and used for bedding for the stock who would need to move into barns over the cold months. Hill farmers over the centuries had been harvesting ferns in this way. Friday night. Bob was watching a box set on the tv. He'd heard it was good and was enjoying it, though there were far too many episodes. He'd have forgotten half of them before it went much further.

He had been busy at work , so got himself a takeaway on the way home. It was ok but nothing like the meals his sister prepared. He really must do another shop. He'd done food for the dogs but although he had his own in the freezer nothing really appealed to him.

He thought of the Sunday lunches he and his sister's family had often shared. 'I'll do one for myself this week-end ' he thought.

At that moment the phone rang. 'Hi, it's me, Jean.' As if he didn't know it.   'We all think it is high time you paid us a visit, so when are you coming? No excuses. The children are missing the dogs.' He laughed. That was followed by 'what are you eating?' 'Takeaway' he said feeling guilty.

'I knew it'. 'Right, it's half term the week after next and I've made plans for us all. He protested he was too busy. He had a kitchen to finish installing. It would take at least another week. However, when pressed he admitted it was probably just a few days' work. So a date was settled on and in bed that night Bob was secretly pleased she had insisted. He and the dogs had missed the family.

Sunday morning was to be a training exercise and dogs and handlers were there. Dusty had been away for well over a month.   Now on his return he seemed different somehow. Charlie was not sure what it was. He didn't like the large dog and kept out of the way. He'd done another successful locate and was telling some of the others about it and how difficult it had been, as again there had been three people in different locations. He'd needed to concentrate hard, especially as the weather had been poor. He'd just stopped talking when he realized he was too close to Dusty. He sniffed. The dog smelled different. What was it? 'Think you're so clever don't you the other dog snarled, Well I've news for you, you aren't.'

Then, with no further ado, he launched himself at Charlie pulling his handler over. A battle royal commenced. A shocked Bob and other handlers eventually managed to separate the two dogs. On inspection Charlie didn't seem badly hurt, but there were several puncture wounds.

Dusty's handler was shocked and apologetic. He knew the dog could have an uncertain temper but he had never acted like this, though he had been off colour for a while. The vet hadn't been able to find anything though so it was a puzzle.

Safely back at home, after being checked over, Charlie thought about what had happened. He couldn't tell Bob but there was something definitely wrong with Dusty. Charlie could smell it. Whatever it was Charlie hoped the dog would soon be better. He told Megan who just said that she had warned him about Dusty but secretly she was really glad Charlie was ok. To prove it she even shared her bone with him. A high honour!

'You were very brave Charlie' his spirit guide told him later that night when everyone had gone to bed, and Charlie was dozing in his basket in the kitchen 'and you were right. He is far from well.'

'About time too' said Jean when the car turned into the drive and Bob and the dogs got out. Casserole. Charlie could smell it instantly. Casserole, his favourite. Peas, carrots, potatoes, meat and added veggies. Just as he liked it. His mouth watered. Jean had been so upset when she learned what had happened that she had decided to make everyone's favourite for tea. Pud was apple pie and custard, not doggy food of course, but she had remembered to put some apples on one side for them. As comfort food went it was ace!

Days flew by. It was just like old times Charlie thought. He loved the new house, in the small village and Alex and Holly's friends. Food wasn't bad either. They had good food at Bob's but Jean added something extra to hers. Even the mince tasted different. He knew he was being made a fuss of and decided to lap it up, as it wouldn't last for long. Megan just sniffed at him.

He didn't think about going back, though he knew he had to and maybe even work with Dusty if it was asked of him. However, he liked this place. It had a lovely comforting smell to it . He loved the fuss too, and the odd visit with Bob to the pub. No one said anything about his appearance Charlie thought and he had forgotten he was different in any way.

CHAPTER FOURTEEN

'Brecon and Monmouthshire Canal, that's where we'll go today.' Jean told them over breakfast on the Saturday morning. 'Your dad is taking us to lunch at the local pub on Sunday, so a good walk now and a short one after lunch tomorrow will be just what we need.'. 'I think we'll save the Brecon Promenade walk and the peddilos until your Uncle Bob's next visit.'

'Do we have to go mum?' grumbled Alex and Holly. Alex saying there was a new game on his x box, and Holly that she wanted to spend time with a school friend. But their mum was firm, 'yes you do. Uncle Bob's going home soon and I want us to enjoy this time together'.

When they arrived they saw little boats taking people on trips along the canal. Some of the boats were being steered by visitors. Others by the men who worked for the pleasure boat company. As the family walked along the towpath they passed quite a few people, families, or lone walkers, mums pushing babies in buggies, dog walkers, photographers, ducks swimming. Even the occasional seagull. On the far bank someone had spotted a heron. It was standing so still that unless you looked very carefully you wouldn't see it. They turned back after about an hour or so.

Both Charlie and Megan were on leads, and Megan was her usual placid self. Charlie was sniffing round not paying particular attention. He was feeling much better, soreness all gone and he greeted the few dogs he saw with his usual friendliness. He was slightly wary when he saw a GSD coming towards him. However, the dog was friendly so all went well. Charlie relaxed.

'We'll stop here for a sandwich and a drink' Jean told everyone, spotting an empty bench, 'then we can walk back to the car. The dogs were lying at Bob's side. He was having a sip of tea and just had a bite of sandwich when his sister asked him what he thought of the area. 'I like it.' He then wondered why she had asked. Sisters never did anything without a good reason (least mine didn't) he thought. What was she up to?

Bob was lost in thought so didn't notice the ducks that were clambering up the bank to his left, searching for food thrown down for them. He didn't but guess who did?

Whether they reminded Charlie of the geese on the farm he never knew, but he suddenly remembered his brothers and sister and the games they had played. He sat absolutely still for a moment then without stopping to think he edged away from Bob his lead trailing and began to stalk them, slowly at first then with longer strides. They were sitting in a circle backs away from him and he was getting closer and closer. Whether they could smell him or something else warned them no one knew but all of a sudden with a commotion they began to waddle back to the water and safety. A nearby seagull was eyeing up the scraps of food greedily. His eyes fixed on Charlie.

Charlie was in his element. A game, he thought, a game. I can round this duck up. As the last one waddled down the bank towards the water the dog began to skirt round it, sure he could stop it. He hadn't lost his old skill after all. He told Megan later he really thought he could get there in time, he always had before.

Unfortunately, he had forgotten the seagull who thinking the food left was going to be taken, suddenly dived at Charlie, squawking noisily, wings outstretched.

It took the dog completely by surprise. The wings beat near his face and for a split instant Charlie was confused. He backed away, forgetting where he was and moved backwards. In horror although Bob yelled 'stop', Charlie couldn't. The edge of the muddy crumbly bank gave way and with a resounding splash he fell into the canal.

Shrieks. Pandemonium everywhere. Phones and cameras on the go, Bob was frantically trying to lean over to grab Charlie's collar without himself falling in. His clothes were now muddy and soaked. Ruined! Chaos reigned.

Finally, one elderly man with a hooked walking stick who had seen what had happened offered his stick to Bob. He managed to hook Charlie's collar with it and drag the soaking, bedraggled dog to the edge of the bank where Bob was able to get him.

It didn't help that Alex and Holly were laughing as in the end was Jean, Stewart and some of the passers by. Safely on dry land Charlie of course did what all dogs who have been in water do. He stood there and shook himself. Droplets of water went everywhere. What made it worse was that Charlie's ignominious dip in the canal was now recorded for posterity.

CHAPTER FIFTEEN

Over lunch the next day in the pub various people came across to say hello and comment on Charlie's exploits. It seemed everybody in the village had heard what had happened. Some hadn't even been there! The elderly man with his stick had though. Bob thanked him again and was told that no thanks were necessary.

Mr. Christopher, for that was the man's name, said that he had been pleased to help. He hated to see any dog in distress especially so since he had recently lost his own dog. Holly asked 'if the dog had died'. 'No, he ran away, and I blame myself. It was all my fault.' Sitting having coffee with them he explained that his niece worked in an animal rescue centre.

Several weeks ago someone had dumped a little dog outside the Centre, 'They tied it up and just left it. No phone call, no note, nothing. There are so many dogs there and there was no space for another. The Rescue called him Barney. So I told my niece I would look after it, temporarily until they could find it a home. He is a lively little thing. To be honest more than I can cope with, but I didn't have the heart to say anything. Thought maybe he would settle down. Jean thought back to Teddy.

By now all the family were listening. ' I was out in an area somewhere near Pen y Fan, several days ago now, walking, with Barney. I didn't want to leave him on his own at home - so unfair. I was taking photos too. 'It's my hobby' he explained, going on to say 'especially planes.' He'd won prizes for his photos.

'Sometimes on The Beacons we see Chinooks fly over, from their local base, but that day it was even better. Totally unexpected. In the distance coming towards me was a large Lockheed Hercules. I couldn't believe it. The perfect shot. Everything was just right, the weather, the time of day, the scenery, the light etc.'

'I don't really remember what happened. All I know is that Barney panicked, ripped the lead out of my hands and ran. I lost my balance and fell. By the time I got to my feet he had disappeared completely. That was almost a week ago and I've not had one day's rest since. I've even been back calling and looking for him, but, of course, how could I expect him to come when he hardly knows me.' Mr. Christopher blew his nose on a large white hankie. It was clear he was very upset, almost in tears.

'I've even asked members of the local Mountain Rescue if they are out on an exercise to keep an eye out for him. Offered a reward too. Keep hoping someone will find him. That little dog has been through so much. First dumped like that, then ending up with me. And now this! I love him to bits, but to be honest I'm not the right one to care for him.' Jean got up and put her arm round Mr. Christopher, before looking at her brother.

Bob sat quietly for a moment before asking if Mr. Christopher had anything of Barney's with him. 'A blanket in the car' was the reply. 'I keep it just in case. Bob asked two questions. 'First may I borrow this? Believe it or not Charlie is becoming a really good search and rescue dog though he's not yet fully trained. 'Well, he's good' he added 'when he's not thinking he can round up the ducks! My other dog Megan is too though she's out of action at the moment.'

' I can't promise anything but Charlie seems to have ESP when it comes to searching for people. He's never looked for a dog but he's still following a scent, so to him although there will be a difference between a person's and an animal's it may be he can do it.'

'We'll need some help though, as it will take more than just me. Can you give me the name of someone you know in Search and Rescue who would go out with me and act as my navigator?' Mr. Christopher nodded. 'I do know of someone and am sure he'll help.'   Bob looked at the family who all agreed how wonderful it would be if Charlie could find Barney. That search came first. They could always go for a walk another time.

'I'll be back in a minute' said Mr. Christopher. He was as good as his word and returned with a tall fair haired young man. 'This is John. He's just finished his shift behind the bar and is more than willing to go with you. He's been a member of Search and Rescue for two years and knows the area quite well. He has Mollie, a young Border Collie. She's still in training but John thinks she will be a great asset to the team.'

The men and Charlie, all kitted out began the walk. Bob had his rucksack, but it was almost empty – just in case it was needed. Yes there were a few essentials but John's had the complete kit.   Charlie with his jacket and light on plus bell sniffed the blanket as they set out. The scenery was beautiful. Bob and John with their work in Search and Rescue found they had a lot to talk about. The area was stunning Bob admitted to himself but both mens' eyes never strayed far from Charlie.

There were loads of scents everywhere especially in the general area near Pen y Fan but not the one Charlie was searching for. He had been alert from the moment Bob had let him sniff the blanket.

Bob had explained to Charlie that this time they were looking for a little dog that was lost somewhere on the Beacons. He is only small and has been badly treated in his previous home so it may be that he is still so terrified he won't respond to you. 'We have to try Charlie, we just have to do our best. What do you think?'

Charlie had gazed at Bob as if he could understand his every word. There was a thoughtful look on the dog's face. He so desperately wanted to please Bob. However, now out on the mountain there was nothing the dog could smell, no scent he could find so what could he do? He suddenly thought of his spirit ancestor. Where was he? He had helped him before but! What was he to do?

The dog stood head to one side as he thought, remembering what his ancestor had told him once before. Trust your nose. Move further away. Listen to what the wind is telling you. He began to cast in wider and wider circles. Moving further away.

'I won't give up' he said to himself. 'I won't. I know he is here and I must find him. It's my job. That's what I am, a search and rescue dog.' He thought of Barney and how terrified the little dog must have been when he ran away. If he was scared then how much more would he be terrified now. All alone. He would have been looking for somewhere safe. Nothing here but in the distance , it seemed like miles away, he could see rocks. Perhaps? He could also smell that peculiar scent, the one he was so desperate to find when first at Bob's.

However, it was at that same moment that any thought of going off to find any other scent but the one he was searching for vanished forever from his mind. 'Find Barney, must find Barney', were the words running through his mind.

'He's onto something' said Bob, 'I can feel it. You ok to carry on?' John nodded. 'Let's go further afield. We just need to keep an eye on the weather.' He thought to himself that Barney could be anywhere. The chances of finding him were slim, but he didn't say anything, thinking that sometimes miracles do happen.

They had been searching now for almost two hours. In that time the weather had begun to close in as folks say, and a fine mist was beginning to appear.

The men looked at each other. Although they didn't want to turn back, maybe it was sensible. 'Charlie', Bob called. Yet just as the dog was beginning to turn away to come back to Bob he caught a faint scent. Ignoring Bob he dashed away . He was following his nose, the scent on the breeze, and he knew he had to find it, to go on until he found it. Where was it? What should he do?

Think Charlie think. Maybe if he closed his eyes and concentrated the idea would come. What had his spirit guide told him. Use all your abilities. Clear your mind of thoughts. Let the thought or picture come in to you. He was still. Suddenly in his mind he could see a pile of rocks or was it stones? They were in the far distance. He opened his eyes and looked again. There almost on the horizon he could see, several smallish rocks. He hadn't noticed them before.

CHAPTER SIXTEEN

Barney was cold, scared and exhausted. His lead was wrapped round him and he had no idea how long he had been lying in the hole. Dogs don't know time as we do, but it seemed forever. When it had rained he had managed to lick a few drops of water as it splashed on the rocks near where he was lying. That kept him alive.

'No-one's going to find me, are they'? His throat was raw from barking. Over the days he had been trapped he had picked up sounds of people in the distance hoping they would hear him and he would be rescued. But no one had come. He would never be found.

Why had he run away? That day when it happened it had been the sound and sight of the big noisy thing in the sky that had made him tremble. Barney had jerked at the lead, pulling it out of the man's hands. When the old man fell suddenly the lead dangled on the ground and Barney just had to run. Run as fast as he could from the scary monster. His mind had shut down but now lying in this cold dark hole with a large grey stone overhead he was remembering the old man's house, the kindness, the warmth, the food etc and he wished, oh how he wished he was back there.

Outside on The Beacons Charlie had dashed away , first in a straight line, before veering to the left - then after a moment. 'Got it'. The large rocks in the distance looked nearer now and the scent was slightly stronger. He paused, paw lifted.

Nothing. Bark, bark he was being told. Barney was out there somewhere. Charlie felt his spirit guide drawing nearer. He was there with him. They would do this together. So he barked. Nothing. He listened, turning his head slightly before barking again.

It was then he heard it, a small timid bark. It was so faint he almost missed it. Charlie barked again, this time a reassuring sound. Again, a faint reply on the wind. He listened for a minute then set off in the direction he thought he heard it.

As he was crossing a gulley it was then he picked up the scent. It was strong now. Much stronger. The men could see the light on Charlie's jacket as he raced ahead. He eventually stopped by the mound of rocks , under which was a hole. It was here the scent was strongest. Lying down he barked, gently this time. A tiny bark came back in reply. He'd found him. He'd found Barney.

CHAPTER SEVENTEEN

'I'm stuck' said Barney. 'I've tried to get out but my lead has twisted and my back leg hurts. It doesn't work properly. I tried barking but no-one heard me. I've been so scared. Please don't leave me all on my own'.

'I have to go but I promise you I'll be back. I promise.' They were the last words Barney heard as Charlie raced back across the Beacons towards Bob and John. He raced up to Bob almost jumping up, and barked. He did this several times, eyes alert, tongue hanging out as if to say 'look what I've found, come and see now. Look what I've found. I've found him'.

He didn't know how to tell Bob that Barney was hurt. Then he thought. He held up a back leg and limped. He looked up at Bob as if willing him to understand. 'What on earth' Bob thought. A moment ago Charlie was hurtling full speed towards him. Now he was acting as if he had been hurt.

'If I didn't know any better' John said 'I'd think he was trying to tell us that Barney is hurt'.

Somehow Barney had managed to become wedged in the hole, unable to move. Both men struggled to get a grip but the rock was smooth. What on earth were they to do? They couldn't leave the little dog and even if they stayed with him and radioed for help it would be ages before anyone arrived with the necessary tools to help dig the dog out.

It was then Charlie said later to Megan that he had what people call a 'light bulb moment'. As he sat and watched the men he suddenly remembered digging in that garden to try and stretch the wire by the roses. Dig. That's what he needed to do. So, sticking his head in front of Bob he began to dig with his front paws. The ground was hard and his paws became sore but still he continued to dig. Until suddenly Bob saw earth come away.

'Leave Charlie' he told the dog and he and John renewed their efforts to move the rock. At last they felt it give a little. It was still a struggle but the men managed to get Barney out. As they lifted him clear the dog began to whine. It was evident he was in pain. They saw his left leg was hanging limply. 'Broken I reckon' said John.

The little dog was thin and tired, but so happy to see them and licked first Bob, then John. Although Barney was shaking he was clearly delighted to be found. Charlie danced about in joy and happiness, barking and barking. Bob carefully wrapped Barney in the blanket and put him in his rucksack. He needed to be careful going back down to the car and kept talking to Barney telling him he would be home soon and that everything would be all right. On the way down John commented that he wished he had put a Fido Pro in his pack for Charlie whose paws were cracked. That way the dog could have been carried down safely too.

John rang a delighted, overwhelmed Mr. Christopher who was waiting at home in the hope there would be good news. His niece Sarah was with him. He left it to him to spread the good news to Jean and family. Search and Rescue had already been told.

At the car park Mr. Christopher and his niece were waiting, ready to take Barney straight to the emergency vet. An out of hours practice had agreed to check the dog over. Never mind the expense. Barney's guardian was so grateful the little dog was safe and sound. In the end both dogs were seen by the vet. Charlie's sore paws were treated and a special antiseptic cream given to Bob for them.

Barney did have a broken leg, and was dehydrated. So, before anything else was done bloods were taken to make sure that his organs were all right. The vet needed to find out whether Barney was anaemic etc.

First of all the shock needed to be treated before the leg and the little dog was put on a drip. The first level was a shock fluid rate. This would be for roughly 2-4 hours. Then all being well he would then be on a maintenance plus rate. The drip was to be in for some time and Barney would have to stay at the vets probably for a few days to be monitored.

However, his vital signs appeared good, so with any luck he wouldn't have to stay in too long. So, then water was offered, and a tiny amount of food. It was clear however that the dog was exhausted and needed to sleep. Sometimes sleep is the best medicine whether for people or animals. Mr. Christopher and his niece went home happily, after thanking all concerned for Barney's safe recovery. At Jean's after a hot drink and a warm meal John and Bob were bombarded by questions from Alex and Holly.

Charlie the hero of the hour, just sat quietly, beaming. Jean had given Charlie chicken and veggies with a special gravy. He had earned it. In his heart was a feeling he couldn't identify. Yes he had found Barney but the feeling was throughout his body and so much more than the pride he knew at doing a good job. The job he was trained for. What was it? **Do you know?**

Megan was slightly put out when she realised what she had missed, but then thought how well Charlie had done. She wasn't sure she would have been able to find Barney. She was still slightly under the weather because of the arthritis . So with a sigh she settled into her basket by the fire – much nicer!

Bob didn't say a great deal. His heart was too full. Pride in Charlie's achievement was uppermost. In bed that night he thought about his dog and his own pride in him. Yes, although he was proud to be Charlie's guardian what mattered most was that this remarkable dog had focused his all in finding Barney.

CHAPTER EIGHTEEN

Cameras and iPhones were at the ready as loads and loads of photos were taken, including several group ones.   A beaming Mr. Christopher insisted on handing over the promised reward to Bob. That however was going straight to the local Search and Rescue team.   They were a charity and funds were low, and Bob had a feeling, a funny feeling, that maybe before too long he and Charlie might become part of that team.

He thought of Megan. She was really too old now to be out on Search and Rescue work: that required a younger dog especially in bad weather.   So from now on apart from walks etc Megan's place would be in her basket by the fire.   Now it was Charlie's turn to do her job and step up to the mark.

The day wasn't over yet though. Another surprise, an unexpected one, was still to come. Tea in the local village hall was 'awesome' as Alex and Holly told friends later. We all had to dress up.

Would the request for 'just one more photo please' ever stop? First of all there was one of Charlie, with little Barney, whose left leg contrary to all expectations was not in plaster. These days unless it was a serious break high up the leg, pins or perhaps a plate would be inserted, over that would be a covering bandage.

Jean, Stewart and family including Charlie of course, had visited Mr. Christopher, and Barney several times since the little dog had been back at home. Mr. Christopher was now called Martin by Jean, Stewart and Bob. To the children he was Uncle Martin. In fact he almost felt like another Uncle.

Today, all photos showed a transformed bright eyed Barney. He'd been carefully showered and groomed to perfection.

Pongy shampoo thought Charlie but he didn't really mind. The look on the little dog's face seemed to say 'my hero'. Charlie was then presented with the largest, shiniest medal he had ever seen. This called for yet more photos. 'You ought to have him on Facebook' someone told Bob, who just shook his head. No thanks he thought that wasn't for them.

'Now before we all have tea', Mr Christopher said 'there's something else I'd like to say. Stewart, Jean Alex, and Holly.' He beckoned them forward. The children looked puzzled. What was happening?

'As you know I don't feel I am the right person to be Barney's guardian. He needs someone who will play with him, take him for long walks, and make sure he is part of a family. I've talked things over with your mum and dad, and my niece.'

There was silence. 'I am delighted to say that your parent have agreed now's the time to have a family dog. Who better than Barney? What do you say?' Alex and Holly stared at their parents before flinging their arms around them, a delighted Martin Christopher and an even more delighted Barney. He didn't normally do hugs, or know exactly what was happening but whatever it was felt good.

Mr, Christopher raised his glass and said, 'so, before we all tuck into tea, let's say thank you once more to Charlie. Without him we wouldn't be here celebrating today.'

So, Well Done
Charlie
Well Done